The Shepherds' Song

CREATED AND PRODUCED BY

Dennis & Nan Allen

Drama and Lyrics by Nan Allen • Music and Arrangements by Dennis Allen

Orchestrated by Dave Williamson

Companion Products Available:

Listening Cassette 0-7673-9242-6
(Listening Cassettes available in quantities of ten or more for $3.00 each
from your Music Supplier or Genevox Music Group)

Listening CD 0-7673-9243-4

Accompaniment Cassette 0-7673-9244-2
(Side A: Split-track / Side B: Instruments only)

Accompaniment CD 0-7673-9248-5 (Split-track only)

Orchestration 0-7673-9046-6

Cassette Promo Pak 0-7673-9247-7

CD Promo Pak 0-7673-9245-0

Instrumentation includes: Flute 1-2, Oboe, Clarinet 1-2, Trumpet 1-2-3,
French Horn 1-2-3, Trombone 1-2-3, Tuba, Drum Set, Percussion,
Timpani, Harp, Rhythm, Violin, Viola, Cello, String Bass
Substitute Parts: Alto Sax 1-2-3 (substitute for French Horn 1-2-3),
Tenor Sax/Baritone Treble Clef (substitute for Trombone 1-2),
Clarinet 3 (substitute for Viola), Bass Clarinet (substitute for Cello),
Bassoon (substitute for Cello), Keyboard String Reduction

GENEVOX

FOREWORD

What exactly is "peace?" The Bible tells us that Jesus was the Prince of Peace, but what does that mean in our everyday lives? *The Shepherds' Song* tells the story of that search in the lives of two shepherds, Eli and Jacob. Through their search we relive the events of Jesus' holy birth and, along the way, we discover the source of peace in our own hearts.

The music and the story are familiar, but we pray that your encounter with the Lord is fresh and meaningful.

Dennis & Nan Allen

SEQUENCE

Processional

Arranged by Dennis Allen

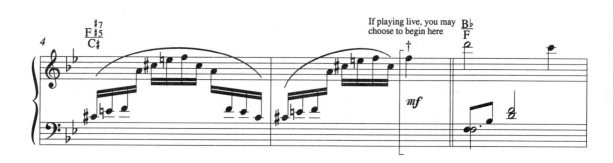

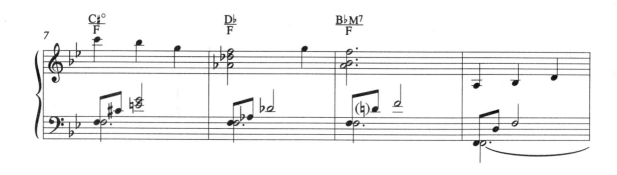

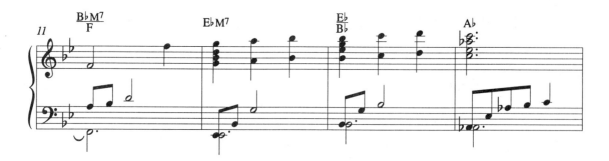

†"It Came upon the Midnight Clear," Words by EDMUND H. SEARS. Music by RICHARD STORES WILLIS.

†"The First Nowell," Traditional English Carol.

†"While Shepherds Watched Their Flocks," Words by NAHUM TATE. Music by GEORGE FREDERICK HANDEL.

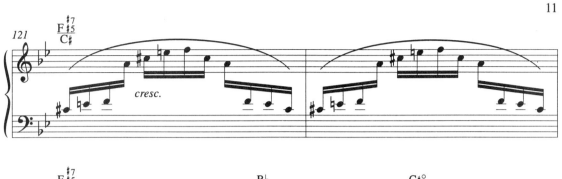

NARRATOR: The word went out over all the land...a new law handed down from the Caesar himself, "all the world shall be taxed and counted in a census." And all went to their own ancestral homes in compliance with the Roman law.

And Joseph, a carpenter, left his home in Nazareth of Galilee...and traveled to the city of David...known as Bethlehem. And he brought with him his wife, Mary, who was about to give birth to a Child.

(lights up on manger scene at stage left)

And it happened that while they were in Bethlehem...the Baby was born. Mary wrapped the Baby Boy in swaddling clothes and laid Him in a manger in a stable, because they could find no other place to stay.

Immediate segue to "God Rest Ye Merry, Gentlemen"

God Rest Ye Merry, Gentlemen

Traditional Carol
Arranged by Dennis Allen

Driving, in two (♩ = ca. 86)

MEN unis. *f*
God rest ye mer - ry, gen - tle - men; let

LADIES unis. *f*
Re - mem - ber Christ, our

noth - ing you dis - may.

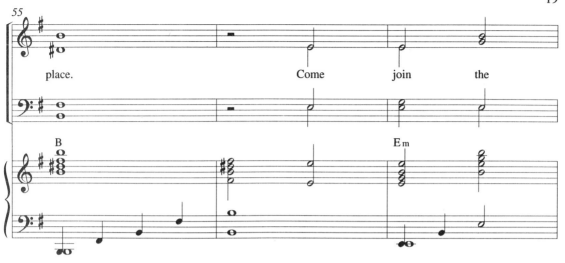

place. Come join the

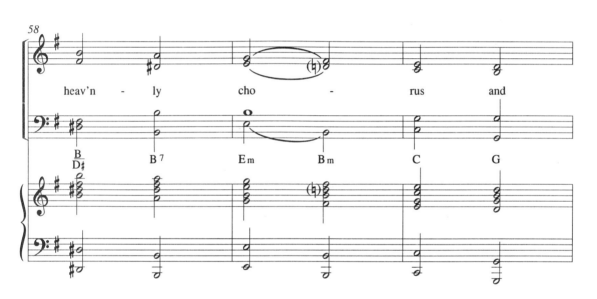

heav'n - ly cho - rus and

sing the Fa - ther's praise.

20

com - fort and joy!

24

(lights down on manger scene)

NARRATOR: And so it was that there were shepherds living in the fields nearby, and they were watching over their sheep at night...

SCENE I

(lights up on shepherds' campsite at stage right)
(Scene opens as the two shepherds are sitting by the fire. Jacob is playing a flute.)

ELI: Jacob...must you play that noise...constantly? You're keeping the sheep awake...and you're annoying me!

JACOB: What, old man? You don't like my music?

ELI: That's not music. And no, I do not like it. It's...common...and loud.

JACOB: Well, you're common...and I'm loud! *(laughing hysterically)* *(continues playing)*

ELI: Hush! They can hear you all the way to the marketplace in Bethlehem.

JACOB: Oh, Eli. Bethlehem's at least a mile or more from here. And besides, the wind is blowing from the west tonight carrying my song to...to...let's see, we are east of Bethlehem and the wind blows from west to east...and...east of here...is...

ELI: ...the dead sea

JACOB: How about that...my song falls only on...dead ears!

ELI: That's the only thing it's fit for.

JACOB: What's the matter, old man? I'm just trying to pass the time. Watching sheep is quite boring.

ELI: *(indignant)* Our forefather...the great shepherd...David...did not think it boring. He considered it an honor to keep the flocks that would one day become sacrifice in the temple in Jerusalem.

JACOB: Perhaps. But David passed the time away with music, too.

ELI: Well, David, passed the time playing real music...the harp...the beautiful, peaceful harp.

JACOB: *(making strumming sounds)* Brmmm! Brmmmm! Brmmmm! *(etc.)* Oh, you're right, Eli. I am at such peace now.

(Jacob laughs hysterically again)

ELI: What do you know of peace? *(almost under his breath)* In my day, young men had respect for their elders...

JACOB: Times have changed, Eli.

ELI: Yes, they have. And if you ask me, Rome is to blame! Those Romans have corrupted the young minds of Judean boys.

JACOB: You think so?

ELI: I do. But when our Savior comes...He will lift up the humble and crush the proud! He will give power to the righteous. Finally, there will be peace in our land.

JACOB: Peace through power? You're dreaming, old man. Prosperity. Now there's something that will bring us peace. Money flowing into our pockets.

ELI: Oh, listen to the wild dreams of a poor shepherd.

JACOB: I may not always be a shepherd, Eli. Did you ever think of that?

ELI: It's just that your father was a poor shepherd...your grandfather was a poor shepherd...

JACOB: But that doesn't mean I will always be a shepherd. No, I'll move on to greater things one day and if the Savior comes...

ELI: If?

JACOB: All right, when the Savior comes, He will be like Solomon, the great King. Gold and silver will run like rivers in the streets. And who will be downstream to collect it?

ELI: You, I suppose?

JACOB: Who else?

ELI: You have it all wrong, young Jacob. Our Savior will care nothing of wealth. He will be like the great warrior, David. He will command on a white horse and carry the sword of victory. He'll slay those Roman oppressors and there will be peace.

JACOB: Peace with a sword. What an idea! No, old man. Money is more powerful than the blade.

ELI: The Prince of Peace will grant us power.

JACOB: He will bring us prosperity...

(lights down on campsite)

Who Shall Come?

Words and Music by
DENNIS and NAN ALLEN
Arranged by Dennis Allen

FIRST TIME: choir unison
SECOND TIME: ladies

1. Who shall come, who shall take the throne___
2. Who shall come, who shall set us free___

28

(lights up on campsite)
(Scene reopens as Jacob is playing a sad song on his flute)

ELI: You play a mournful song now, Jacob. What happened to the happy tune?

JACOB: Oh, I don't know. Sometimes I feel a little sad. Is that so wrong?

ELI: What will make you happy, then, Jacob?

JACOB: I told you. Fame and fortune.

ELI: Now, it's fame and fortune.

JACOB: Well, I could do without the fame. I'm not that greedy.

ELI: And how do you plan to achieve these ridiculous things?

JACOB: I don't know...yet.

ELI: Perhaps you will be a world renowned musician, eh?

JACOB: Maybe. But whatever I do, I'll find favor with kings and rich people and the palace historians will write about me. Yes...I can see it now.

ELI: Oh? Can you see that the sheep you are suppose to be watching...are straying from the sheepfold...wandering off into the night?

JACOB: What?

ELI: It's your watch. It's your turn to sleep in the door of the sheepfold.

JACOB: Oh, no! Oh, yes, it is. Sorry, Eli...uh until morning then...good night.

(Jacob exits)

ELI: *(mumbling under his breath)* That boy...not a good shepherd...*(lying down to sleep)* his dreams are wild and he has no idea about the Savior...the mighty Prince of Peace.

(lights on campsite remain up, but dim)

Shepherds' Song

with
Sheep May Safely Graze

Arranged by DENNIS ALLEN

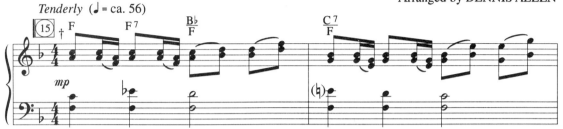

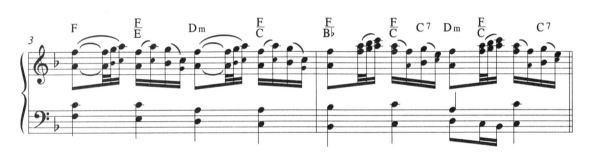

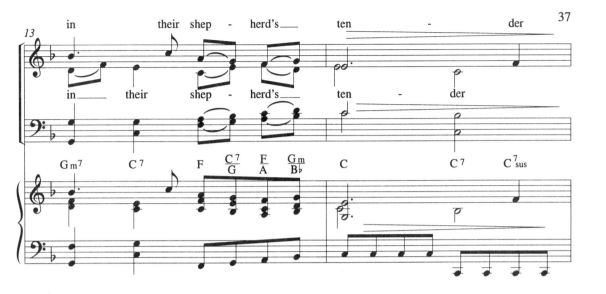

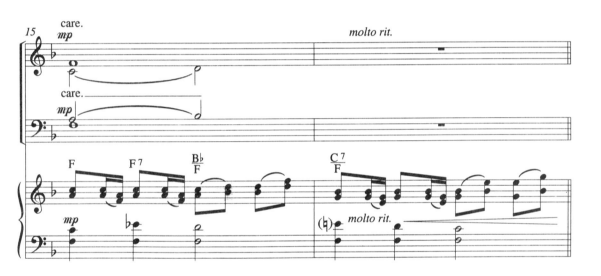

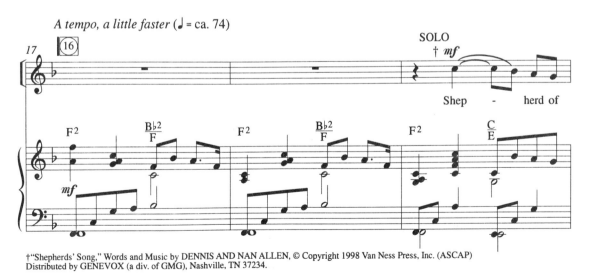

More movement (♩ = ca. 80)

55

Keep me from the en - e - mies, keep me free___ from___

Bb C/Bb Am7 Dm7 Gm7 F/A Gm/Bb

58

unis.
Lead me in - to pas - tures green,

harm.

Csus C Cm7 F F/Eb Bb2/D Gm7

61

div.
lead me to the cool - ing spring, Lead me to the

Cm7 F7 Bb2 Bb Gm7 F/A

Shep - herd of shep - herds,

lead me safe - ly home.

Tidings of Great Joy

Words and Music by
DENNIS and NAN ALLEN
Arranged by Dennis Allen

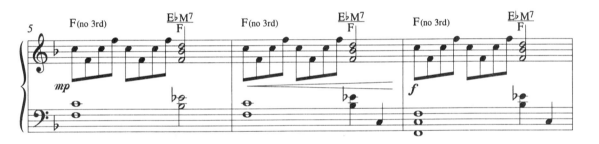

SCENE II

*ELI: *(waking)* What? Morning already? It was a short night...

JOSEPH: *(entering)* Too short.

ELI: *(fully awake)* Wait. Jacob. Look, it is night!

JACOB: It is! It's night...everywhere except where we're standing. How can that be?

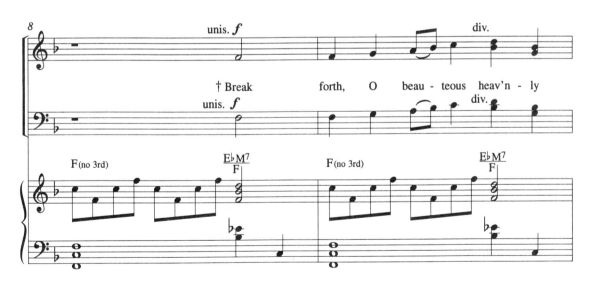

†"Break Forth, O Beauteous Heavenly Light," Words by JOHANN RIST, tr. JOHN TROUTBECK.

hear the an - gel's_____ warn - ing.

Dm   Am   Cm   Gm

Slower (♩ = ca. 74) (♩ = ♩)

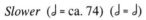

SOLO (male preferably)
mf

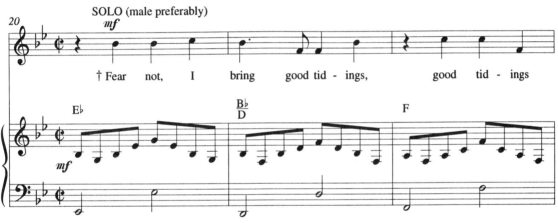

† Fear not, I bring good tid - ings, good tid - ings

E♭   B♭/D   F

of great joy to all. For un - to you is born this

B♭ F/A Gm F E♭   B♭/D

†Luke 2:10-14, Adapted.

day in the ci - ty of Da - vid,

A Sav - ior,_____ who is Christ the Lord._____

JACOB: Did he say...a Savior?
ELI: Yes.
(shepherds begin to relax and look up)

And

A little slower (♩ = ca. 68)

this shall be a sign, you shall find the ba - by

CHOIR
mp

This shall be a sign,

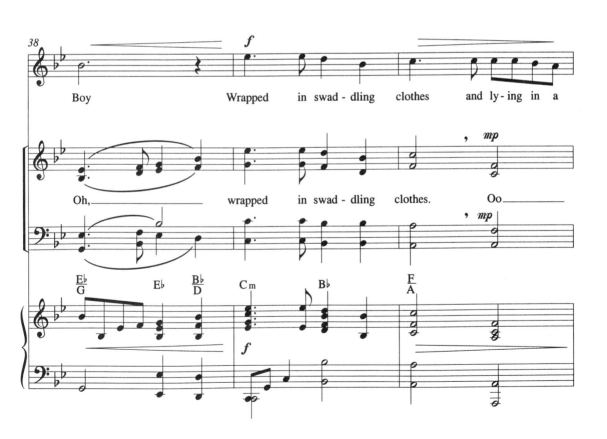

Boy Wrapped in swad - dling clothes and ly - ing in a

Oh,_____ wrapped in swad - dling clothes. Oo_____

*Dialogue begins

man - ger.

JACOB: A manger?
ELI: Yes...a manger!
            (lights flood the set)
JACOB: I've never seen anything so...so...magnificent.
ELI: Angels...they're angels!
JACOB: Angels...everywhere!

Glo - ri - a   in ex -

Glo - ri - a

Shepherd's Jubilee

Arranged by Dennis Allen

SCENE III

(Scene opens as Jacob is quickly packing his bag, music begins)

ELI: Where do you think you're going, Jacob? Why are you packing your bag?

JACOB: What do you think? I'm going to Bethlehem. You heard the angel.

ELI: Of course I heard. But if we both go, who will tend the sheep?

JACOB: *(pause)* The sheep will be safe, Eli. They will be cared for. I'm sure of it...and so are you.

ELI: You're right, Jacob. It'll be light soon. We should leave at dawn.

JACOB: Oh, the city is probably already bursting with excitement. Imagine, the Savior has come!

ELI: Let's not wait until it gets light. Let's go now!

JACOB: Yes...I agree.

(as they exit, conversation fades)

ELI: Now the first thing we should do when we get there is...

JACOB: Why do you get to decide what we do first...

ELI: I'm older and wiser...

JACOB: So what does that matter?

ELI: *(good naturedly)* Ah, Jacob, you never give up, do you?

(shepherds exit)

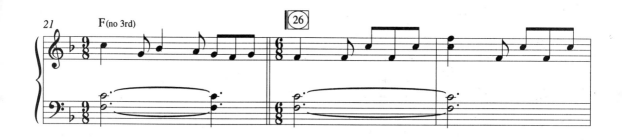

†"Angels We Have Heard on High," Traditional French Carol.

Ma - ry's call - ing; "Hush, hush, qui - et - ly now He slum - bers.

Hush, hush, qui - et - ly now He sleeps."

28 1st time
29 2nd time

SCENE IV

(Scene opens with Abigail and Miriam entering the Bethlehem marketplace at center stage)

MIRIAM: Good morning, Abigail. You're out early today.

ABIGAIL: I like to come to market before the crowds get here.

MIRIAM: Looks like you found some nice produce.

ABIGAIL: Yes, nice. But overpriced. It's robbery, is what it is! Robbery. These pomegranates cost twice as much today as they did last week.

MIRIAM: You should have bartered, Abigail. Bethlehem merchants will always barter.

ABIGAIL: I'm not very good at that. Not as good as you, Miriam.

MIRIAM: Well, it probably wouldn't help to barter today anyway what with the Roman census bringing so many foreigners to our streets. Our merchants know that hungry travelers will pay any amount they ask.

ABIGAIL: Yes, where do you suppose all of these people are from anyway?

MIRIAM: Oh, Galilee, Samaria, maybe. Even as far away as Phoenicia, I suspect. The decree went out to every land that each man should return to his ancestral home. There are Jews living everywhere these days.

ABIGAIL: That means that some will have to travel hundreds of miles to their ancestral home.

MIRIAM: Indeed. But Caesar obviously does not care about the inconvenience. He wants his power...and our money!

ABIGAIL: It's disgraceful.

(enter shepherds into marketplace, hurriedly, excitedly)

ELI: Jacob, slow down. I'm out of breath.

JACOB: Come on, old man. We'll miss the celebration. What if they present the King in a public ceremony this morning and we miss it. Let's go.

ELI: Wait. Aren't you forgetting something?

JACOB: What?

ELI: We don't know where to find the Savior. The angel wasn't so specific as to give us an address.

JACOB: Don't you think that we'll recognize it when we see it? There'll be so much commotion I'm sure we can't miss it.

ELI: Let's at least stop and ask someone before we go running all over town. Here, let's ask these women. *(crossing to Miriam and Abigail)* Excuse us, ladies. Where is the presentation of the Savior to be held?

MIRIAM: Presentation of the...Savior?

ABIGAIL: I think you made a wrong turn in Rome, sir. This is Bethlehem. You won't find any saviors here.

JACOB: He means where do we find the great Prince of Peace?

MIRIAM: A prince? Do you see any palaces?

ABIGAIL: Miriam, it's because we look so royal ourselves...like princesses, don't you think?

MIRIAM: Of course. The elegant clothes we're wearing probably gave us away.

JACOB: Surely you heard the messenger and saw the heavens open up and the sky filled with angels.

MIRIAM: *(incredulously)* Angels. *(trying to escape)* Abigail, I think I hear our husbands calling us.

ABIGAIL: You do? Oh...oh...uh, yes you do. Sorry, sirs, we cannot help you.

MIRIAM: Good day...

ELI: But...

(Abigail and Miriam exit hurriedly)

JACOB: I don't understand. Those women don't seem to know what we're talking about.

ELI: Yes, that is strange. *(enter Man, crossing left to right)* Here's another person. Excuse us, sir. Uh...we were wondering where the presentation of the Savior will be held. Sir...sir...excuse me, sir.

(Man looks at Eli puzzled, but walks on by, exits)

JACOB: He just walked on by. What's the matter with these people? *(enter Woman, crossing right to left)* Miss...uh...miss...we're looking for the Prince.

(Woman ignores Jacob, walks on by, exits)

ELI: She ignored you, Jacob. Just as the gentleman did me. *(pause)* Look at these people here. They're all going about their business as if nothing has happened.

JACOB: A normal day in the marketplace. Have we made a mistake, Eli? Are we in the wrong city...at the wrong time.

ELI: The angel said the Savior was born this day...in the City of David... Bethlehem...

JACOB: And that we would find Him wrapped in swaddling lying...*(suddenly remembers)* lying...in...a...manger.

ELI: Yes, in a stable! That's what the angel said.

JACOB: Then that's where we should start looking...in stables...every stable in Bethlehem if we have to.

ELI: I'm right behind you, Jacob.

(music begins)

(lights down on marketplace)
(Jacob and Eli exit)

Little Town

Words and Music by
DENNIS and NAN ALLEN
Arranged by Dennis Allen

1. O___ lit - tle town___ of
(2. O)___ lit - tle town___ of

Beth - le - hem, an - cient is___ your name. To -
Beth - le - hem, hum - ble on___ the earth. To -

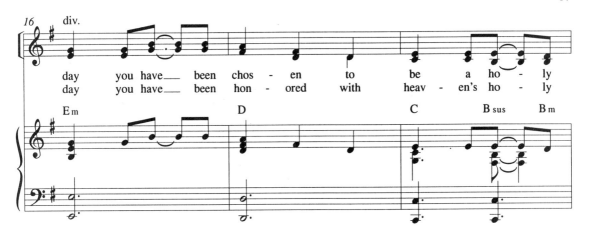

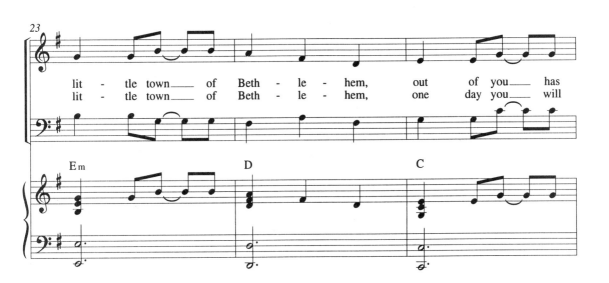

†"O Little Town of Bethlehem," Words by PHILLIPS BROOKS, Music by LEWIS H. REDNER.

Silent Night

Traditional Carol
Arr. by Dennis Allen

NARRATOR: And so...they found Him, not by a sign that directed them...not by
the commotion that surrounded Him...but by their obedience to seek Him.
They found the stable...they found the mother...her husband,...and the Baby
who was lying in a manger...just as the angel had said.
(lights up on manger)
(during song Jacob and Eli cross to manger scene at left, they kneel before the Child.)

SCENE V

(Scene opens as Jacob and Eli are leaving the manger scene crossing back to their "fields") (Jacob is playing a happy tune)

ELI: *(slightly annoyed)* Jacob.

JACOB: What? Does my music annoy you still?

ELI: *(good naturedly)* No, actually...it does not. Now you play it from a heart of joy...which makes it somewhat...*(trying to be polite)* pleasant.

JACOB: *(laughing)* What happened, Eli? What are we feeling?

ELI: I am not sure we will ever understand all these feelings, Jacob.

JACOB: Do you believe it ? Do you believe we saw Him? We actually saw Him!

ELI: Yes...we did.

JACOB: Never in my wildest dreams...

(enter Miriam and Abigail)

MIRIAM: So.

JACOB: Ah, ladies. Good day.

MIRIAM: Did you find your...savior?

ELI: Why yes, as a matter of fact...

ABIGAIL: Was He the Prince of Peace you had envisioned?

JACOB: Well, no...He wasn't.

MIRIAM: No? Well, now you admit it. It was a joke...or was it a dream?

ELI: Neither, my lady. We found the Savior, but He was not the Prince of Peace we had hoped for.

MIRIAM: I'm not surprised.

JACOB: He was...more...than we had hoped for.

ABIGAIL: What? I don't understand.

ELI: I had expected the Prince of Peace to be like our father, David...a mighty warrior who would conquer our enemies and bring us peace.

JACOB: And I thought He would be like the rich King Solomon, who would raise us from our poverty into prosperity and that would bring us peace.

MIRIAM: And He wasn't that at all?

ELI: No, not at all. Instead He was tiny...and lowly...and different. And somehow I...well...we know in our hearts that He came not to bring us peace...but to <u>be</u> our peace.

MIRIAM: Oh, I see...

JACOB: I have spent my whole life hoping that the Savior would come and change the world...my world. Instead, I believe that He came to change...me.

(slight pause)

MIRIAM: Abigail, do you hear our husbands calling us?

ABIGAIL: No, Miriam, I do not.

MIRIAM: Good. Neither do I. *(pause)* Sir, could you show us where we might find this...Savior?

ELI: Indeed...

JACOB: And bring your husbands...*(as they exit)* and your children...and your neighbors, too.

ELI: Come...come and see...

(lights up at manger)
(All cross to manger at left, during narration, shepherds and ladies marvel at the Child. Add other townspeople, if desired)

(music begins)

Peace Will Come

TERRY YORK

DAVID DANNER
Arranged by Dennis Allen

*NARRATOR: The shepherds' new song was a beautiful story...one they told to everyone they met. And all who heard their story were amazed...and many of them believed.

At last their search for peace ended. In Bethlehem they found peace in its truest form. The Prince of Peace had come...and He began to rule in the kingdom of their hearts.

†"Go, Tell It on the Mountain," Traditional Carol

Thou Didst Leave Thy Throne

EMILY E. S. ELLIOTT

TIMOTHY R. MATTHEWS
Arr. by Dennis Allen

With feeling, out of tempo

Lord, You left Your throne and Your king- ly crown, When You came to earth for me. But in Beth - le- hem's home was there found no room For Your ho- ly na- tiv- i- ty. O come to my heart, Lord Je - sus, There is room in my heart for You.

Segue to "Finale"

Finale

With energy ♩ = ca. 76

Arr. by Dennis Allen

†"O Sing a Song of Bethlehem," Words by LOUIS F. BENSON, Music by DENNIS ALLEN, © Copyright 1998 Van Ness Press, Inc. (ASCAP)
Distributed by GENEVOX (a div. of GMG), Nashville, TN 37234.

© Copyright 1998 Van Ness Press, Inc. (ASCAP)
Distributed by GENEVOX (a div. of GMG), Nashville, TN 37234.

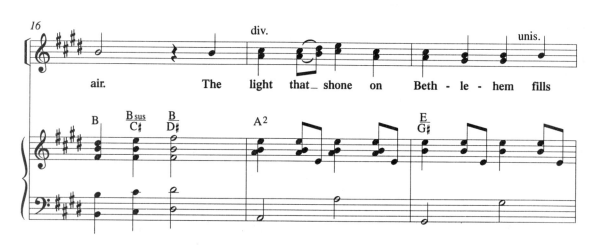

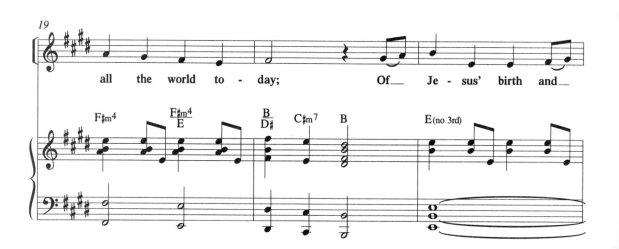

98

†"Joy to the World! The Lord Is Come," Words by ISAAC WATTS, Music by GEORGE FREDERICK HANDEL

PRODUCTION NOTES

CHARACTERS

NARRATOR   An offstage voice or a character on stage who may or may not be a part of the biblical scenes

ELI   An old shepherd. Eli is a "seasoned" shepherd. And with his experience, he is quite intolerant of other ways of thinking. He condescends to his co-shepherd, Jacob, because of Jacob's youth. Eli is from the "old school," and he expects Messiah to deliver the people from Roman oppression by being a mighty warrior.

JACOB   A young shepherd. Jacob taunts Eli and teases him about being old and out of touch. Being from the younger generation, Jacob expects Messiah to deliver him from his position as a poor shepherd and bring riches and prosperity to the land.

ANGEL   A male. The angel has no spoken lines, but has a vocal solo. It is not essential for this character to appear in white raiment and wings. If you choose, the angel's voice may come from offstage and bright lighting may be used to give the illusion of an angel visitation.

MIRIAM   A villager in Bethlehem.
ABIGAIL   A villager in Bethlehem.

MAN   (non-speaking)
WOMAN   (non-speaking)
VILLAGERS   (at least 2) (non-speaking)

MARY   (non-speaking)
JOSEPH   (non-speaking)
WISEMEN   (optional)

SET

If the choir will be in a traditional choir loft and the pulpit area is used for the stage, the following set up will work.

At stage right, the shepherds' campfire may be set. This area may include: stones (real, or made of hard foam), a campfire (created by nailing or gluing wood pieces to a square wooden base; a light inside the assembled wood can make it seem to glow), optional foliage (small shrubbery to frame the set)

At center stage, the Bethlehem marketplace may be set. This area may include: a small "open" tent (colorful fabric with four-poles) , a merchandise cart (wooden with at least two wheels)

At stage left, the traditional manger scene should be set. A crèche (stable shell) may be assembled or a manger with a simple free-standing backdrop would do. A rugged looking backdrop may easily be made by hanging ragged burlap on a three-poled frame...the center pole may be higher than the other two. This gives the nativity scene a "warmth" that a bare stage cannot do. Hang lanterns and put feeding buckets around this set for effect.

COSTUMES

Traditional biblical. Patterns may be bought from McCalls or Simplicity pattern books. Shepherds should look rugged and weather-beaten. The angel may be dressed in white robe. (See character list for options) The villagers should wear brighter colors. Women should wear head pieces. If wise men are used in the finale, their costumes should be colorful and fancy.

The narrator (if on stage) need not be dressed in biblical costume. However, the narrator may, indeed, be a biblical character and wear period costume.

PROPS

a recorder (a small wooden musical instrument)
shepherds' staffs and crooks
fabric bags (two, perhaps made of burlap or heavy fabric)
baskets (two, for villagers)
fruits, vegetables, other merchandise
optional: Wise Men gifts (three...gold, frankincense, myrrh)

STAGING SUGGESTIONS AND PERFORMANCE OPTIONS

The "flute" tune may be performed live on a recorder. The score for each of three tunes is included in this book. If the actor who plays Jacob chooses to mime the tune, you will find it recorded at CD points 52, 53, 54 on the accompaniment track.

Stage lighting may be used to create a dramatic effect. Many stage lighting rental houses will rent and install temporary lighting for a reasonable fee. Most of the lighting consultants can suggest colored gels for the units that will create the effect you want for a scene. They may also suggest some gobos (metal patterns placed in front of a light that will give a special effect, i.e. leaf patterns for outdoors, angels for the visitation scene, etc..) Special bright lights on the shepherds during the angels' visitation scene may give the shepherds more "motive" to "react fearfully."

Most all of the stage directions are found in the script itself. Here are a few exceptions:

During *Peace Will Come*, Miriam, Abigail, shepherds and townspeople remain in manger scene

During *Finale*, Wise Men may enter at measure 71 and present gifts to Child.